D1119913

caillou®

My Imaginary Friend

Adaptation of the animated series: Sarah Margaret Johanson
Illustrations: CINAR Animation; adapted by Eric Sévigny

Caillou was playing with his friend George.
Caillou really liked George. He was lots of fun
and liked to do all the things Caillou liked to do.
But no one else had ever seen George.

George was special because
he was imaginary and only
Caillou knew him.
"Hey George, let's race!"
Caillou said suddenly.
Mommy and Grandma
watched from the kitchen
window.

Caillou and George were having lots of fun.
"Okay, let's race to the barrel. Ready! Set! Go!"
Caillou shouted and ran across the yard.

Caillou ran so fast he bumped into the barrel.
"I won! I won!" he cheered.
Suddenly there was a crash!

Caillou looked around. The flowerpot that was on top of the barrel had fallen to the ground.
"Oops!" said Caillou, looking down at the mess.
Just then, Rosie called to Caillou. It was lunchtime.

Caillou was worried about what had just happened, but ran into the house for lunch anyway.

Caillou forgot all about the broken flowerpot. Mommy said George could join them for lunch.
Caillou talked about how much fun he had playing with his friend.
"George can run really fast, but I beat him in a race!"
"George sounds like fun, Caillou. Does he live nearby?" Grandma asked.

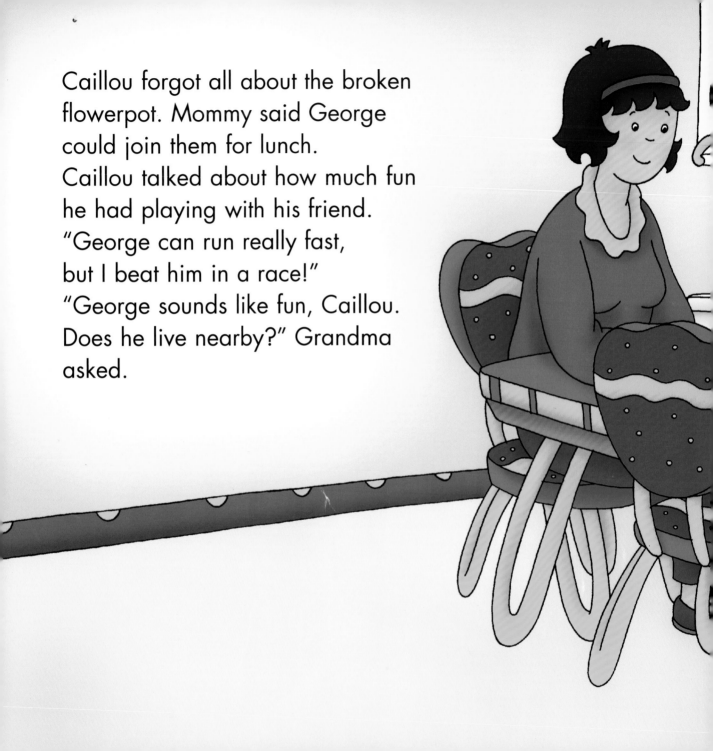

"Um… I think he lives in our basement. George is probably my best friend in the whole world!" Caillou said excitedly. "Caillou, we've all finished eating, and you haven't even touched your food," Mommy said. "Perhaps George could wait outside while you eat your lunch."

"Okay, Mommy," Caillou answered. Caillou got up to move George's chair away from the table so his friend could get down.
"Thank you, George. Caillou will be out soon," Mommy said to Caillou's imaginary friend.

After lunch, Caillou was playing outside again. Daddy was outside too. He was standing by the barrel. "Caillou, would you please come over here for a minute?" Daddy asked.
Caillou walked over to him.

"Do you know anything about this?" Daddy
asked, pointing to the broken flowerpot on
the ground.
Caillou looked down and bit his lip.
"George did it, Daddy," he said. "We were
racing, and he knocked it down."

"Are you sure George did this? Did you have something to do with it too?" Daddy asked in a gentle but serious voice.

Caillou nodded, "Yes, Daddy," he whispered.

"Well, the next time you play with George, you should both be more careful," Daddy said.

"We will, Daddy," Caillou replied.

As Caillou held the dustpan, he said,
"You know, Daddy, George is a bit
clumsy sometimes."
Daddy smiled at Caillou and said,
"A bit like you and me sometimes, right?"
Caillou nodded and smiled back.

© 2009 CHOUETTE PUBLISHING (1987) INC. and COOKIE JAR ENTERTAINMENT INC.
All rights reserved. The translation or reproduction of any excerpt of this book
in any manner whatsoever, either electronically or mechanically and, more
specifically, by photocopy and/or microfilm, is forbidden.

CAILLOU is a registered trademark of Chouette Publishing (1987) Inc.

Text adapted by Sarah Margaret Johanson from the scenario of the CAILLOU animated film
series produced by Cookie Jar Entertainment Inc. (© 1997 CINAR Productions (2004) Inc.,
a subsidiary of Cookie Jar Entertainment Inc.).
All rights reserved.
Original story written by Matthew Cope.
Illustrations taken from the television series CAILLOU and adapted by Eric Sévigny.
Art Direction: Monique Dupras

The PBS KIDS logo is a registered mark of PBS and is used with permission.

We acknowledge the financial support of the Government of Canada through
the Canada Book Fund for our publishing activities.

Canadian   Patrimoine
Heritage   canadien

We acknowledge the support of the Ministry of Culture and Communications
of Quebec and SODEC for the publication and promotion of this book.

SODEC
Québec

Bibliothèque et Archives nationales du Québec and Library and Archives
Canada cataloguing in publication

Johanson, Sarah Margaret
Caillou: my imaginary friend
(Clubhouse)
For children aged 3 and up.

ISBN 978-2-89450-478-9

1. Imaginary companions - Juvenile literature. 2. Friendship - Juvenile
literature. I. Sévigny, Eric. II. CINAR Corporation. III. Title. IV. Title: My
imaginary friend. V. Series.

BF575.F66J63 2004   ¡158.2'5   C2003-941021-8

Printed in Canada
10 9 8 7   CHO1783 APR2011